www.stevecolebooks.co.uk

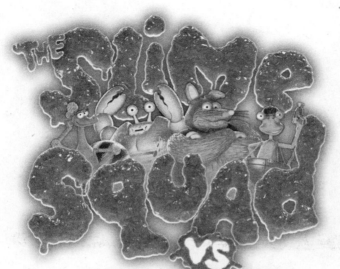

THE SLIME SQUAD

vs

THE CYBER-POOS

by Steve Cole

Illustrated by Woody Fox

RED FOX

THE SLIME SQUAD vs THE CYBER-POOS
A RED FOX BOOK 978 1 862 30878 7

First published in Great Britain by Red Fox,
an imprint of Random House Children's Books
A Random House Group Company

This edition published 2010

1 3 5 7 9 10 8 6 4 2

Copyright © Steve Cole, 2010
Cover illustration and cards © Andy Parker, 2010
Map © Steve Cole and Dynamo Design, 2010
Illustrations copyright © Woody Fox, 2010

The right of Steve Cole to be identified as the author of this work
has been asserted in accordance with the Copyright, Designs and
Patents Act 1988.

The Random House Group Limited supports the Forest Stewardship
Council (FSC), the leading international forest certification
organization. All our titles that are printed on Greenpeace-approved
FSC-certified paper carry the FSC logo. Our paper procurement policy
can be found at www.rbooks.co.uk/environment.

Mixed Sources
Product group from well-managed
forests and other controlled sources
www.fsc.org   Cert no. TT-COC-2139
© 1996 Forest Stewardship Council

Red Fox Books are published by Random House Children's Books,
61–63 Uxbridge Road, London W5 5SA

www.**kids**at**randomhouse**.co.uk
www.**rbooks**.co.uk

Addresses for companies within The Random House Group Limited can
be found at: www.randomhouse.co.uk/offices.htm

THE RANDOM HOUSE GROUP Limited Reg. No. 954009

A CIP catalogue record for this book is available from
the British Library.

Printed in the UK by CPI Bookmaque, Croydon

For Cassie and Nathan

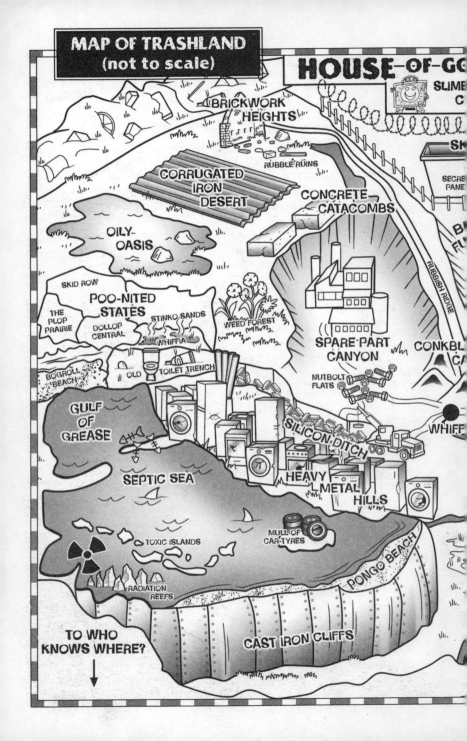

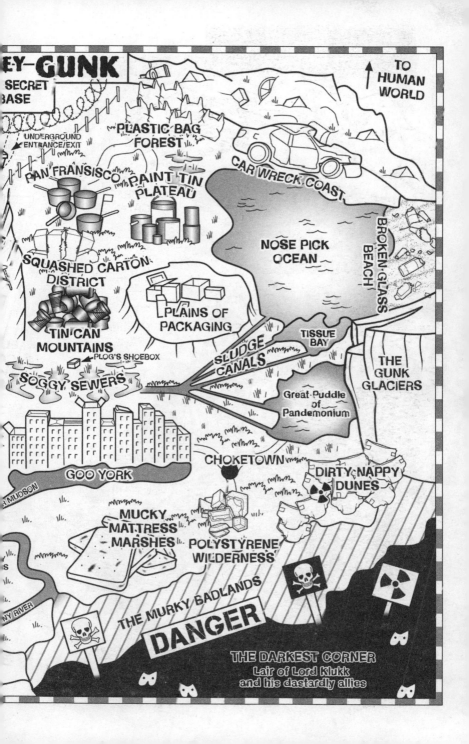

ONCE UPON A SLIME...

The old rubbish dump was far from anywhere. An enormous, mucky, rusty landscape of thousands of thrown-away things.

It had been closed for years. Abandoned. Forgotten.

And then Godfrey Gunk came along.

Godfrey wasn't just a mad scientist. He was a SUPER-BONKERS scientist! And he was very worried about the amount of pollution and rubbish in the world. His dream was to create marvellous mutant mini-monsters out of chemical goo – monsters who would clean up the planet by eating, drinking and generally devouring all types of trash.

So Godfrey bought the old rubbish dump as the perfect testing-ground and got to work.

Of course, he wanted to make good, friendly, peaceful monsters, so he was careful to keep the nastiest, most toxic chemicals separate from the rest. He worked for years and years . . .

And got nowhere.

In the end, penniless and miserable, Godfrey wrecked his lab, scattered his experiments all over the dump, and moved away, never to return.

But what Godfrey didn't know was that long ago, tons of radioactive sludge had been accidentally dumped here. And soon, its potent powers kick-started the monster chemistry the mad scientist had tried so hard to create!

Life began to form. Amazing mini-monsters sprang up with incredible speed.

Bold, inventive monsters, who made a wonderful, whiffy world for themselves from the rubbish around them – a world they named Trashland.

For many years, they lived and grew in peace. But then the radiation reached a lead-lined box in the darkest corner of the rubbish dump – the place where Godfrey had chucked the most toxic, dangerous gunk of all.

Slowly, very slowly, monsters began to grow here too.

Different monsters.

Evil monsters that now threaten the whole of Trashland.

Only one force for good stands against them. A small band of slightly sticky superheroes . . .

The Slime Squad!

Chapter One
STUCK ON YOU!

KER-SPLAT!

In an underground garage in a secret base in the wilds of a whiffy old rubbish dump, a sudden squelch echoed out . . .

And a searing splash of green slime shot past Plog the monster's furry head! Plog dived to the floor, almost squashing his long, rat-like snout on the floor as he did a head-over-heels and bounced back to his feet. KER-SPLOOSH!

Another squirt of slime whizzed between his legs.

"Whoa!" Plog cried, snatching his long, twisty tail out of the way. "Careful, Danjo – this is meant to be just a training exercise, remember?"

"It's only test-slime – not much of a kick!" Danjo Jigg, a crimson crab-creature, grinned from the other side of the garage. "And with the kind of baddies we go up against, training's got to be tough." He waved his rifle in one of his many pincers. "Besides, we've got to test out these new slime-shooters. I can fire hot slime and icy slime from my pincers – but these babies can spray it faster and three times as far!"

"So I noticed,"

Plog puffed, ducking
another high-speed
splat.

But he knew
Danjo was right
about the
enemies they
faced as two
members of the
spectacular Slime
Squad . . .

Trashland, the
abandoned human rubbish-dump that
was now home to millions of mini-
monsters, had always been a peaceful,
pleasant place. But that changed when
evil, mutant mega-monsters started
showing their ugly faces. Born from
ultra-toxic waste in the dump's darkest
corners, led by the mysterious and
villainous Lord Klukk, these sinister
scum-buckets craved total control over
Trashland and its people.

Plog sighed, jumping nimbly to avoid another slime-splat shooting his way. He and his friends were the only ones with enough guts, determination and sheer, slimy super-powers to thwart Klukk and his horrible hench-monsters. But the butt-ugly baddies' plans were growing sneakier and their forces ever stronger – so the Slime Squad was training hard to stay one step ahead . . .

Suddenly – "Argh!" Plog's ears shot up in alarm as he slipped and an extra-hot splodge of slime burst over his nose. "OOF!"

"Gotcha!" Danjo punched a pincer into the air. "The aim was true – now you're wearing the goo!"

"Hooray!" cheered a high, croaky, slightly muffled voice from close by.

Plog wiped the sticky slime from his eyes to find a white frog-monster in round metal pants and a crash helmet apparently jumping out of mid-air. It was Furp LeBurp, hop-about hero and absolute expert on all things slimy – and in actual fact, he was only jumping from the Slime-mobile, the Squad's invisible, all-purpose transport. "HOORAY!" he cried again with a humungous smile on his face.

"You don't have to look so pleased that I've been slime-splattered!" Plog complained.

"Eh? Pardon?" Furp frowned absent-mindedly. "Oh, no, no, no, Plog. I was cheering because I've just invented some fabulous new slimy ammo for the slime-shooters in the lav-lab. This will really help us in the fight against evil."

Plog smiled. The Slime-Mobile's lav-lab was Furp's favourite place – a mobile workshop that was part-toilet, part-laboratory and *all* smelly. "Hang on," he said. "I don't have to get sloshed with this stuff, do I?"

"Nope. It's my turn to play target," said Danjo, tossing him the slime-shooter. He danced and shimmied across the floor on his three sturdy legs. "Bring on the slime – I'll dodge it in time!"

"If you don't, my new 'stick-you' spray will certainly stop you dodging anything else!" Furp loaded the slime-shooter with big, purple bullets. "Aim for his feet, Plog."

Danjo responded by doing a handstand – or rather, a pincer-stand – and waggling his three feet in the air. "Yeah, come on, Plog! Hit them!"

Plog grinned. "I don't think that's quite the test Furp had in mind," he said – and fired at Danjo's right pincer.

"Hey!" Danjo shouted as a purple puddle splashed over his crusty claw. "Not fair!"

Plog winked. "With the kind of baddies we go up against, training's got to be tough!"

Danjo collapsed with a crash. "My pincer's stuck to the floor," he complained.

"My 'stick-you' super-slime works a treat!" Furp cried, jumping about the underground garage, his pants rattling. "Now whenever bad guys attack, we can stop them in their tracks."

"No kidding," Danjo muttered, straining with all his strength to un-stick himself. He squirted red, steaming-hot slime from his claw at the floor, but still the purple goo wouldn't budge.

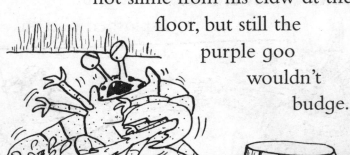

"Let me give you a hand," said Plog. He crossed to join Danjo and grabbed hold of Danjo's pincer. With a grunt of effort he pulled the pincer free – along with a chunk of concrete floor. "Wow, this stuff really is sticky," he realized.

"Thanks, Plog." Danjo smiled. "Er, you can let go of my claw now."

"No, I can't." Plog tried to pull his hand away – and almost yanked Danjo off his feet. "I'm stuck to you!"

"Huh?" Danjo tried to pull away from Plog. Plog tried to pull away from Danjo. It looked like they were having a crazy tug of war. "Furp, what's going on here? Get us unstuck!"

"Oh, dear. Um . . ." Furp looked shifty. "I haven't quite got round to finding a way to un-stick my super-slime."

Plog's eyes narrowed. "You WHAT?"

Furp blushed. "I'm sure it will wear off one day."

"And in the meantime, Plog and I are stuck together?" Danjo groaned. "We're supposed to be tough superheroes. It looks like we're holding hands!"

"Nonsense, my dear Danjo," Furp assured him. "Nobody would think such a thing."

"Er . . . Plog?" came a girlish voice from behind them. "Why are you holding hands with Danjo?"

Furp winced. "Well, almost nobody."

Plog turned to find that the Squad's fourth and final member, Zill Billie, had emerged from the tunnel that led to the group's meeting room. You certainly couldn't call *her* a nobody, he thought fondly. With her bushy black tail, six skinny legs, super-slimy spit and bags of attitude, Zill was like a cool poodle crossed with an atomic skunk – at the moment, a rather worried one.

"We're not holding hands," Danjo insisted, still tugging to be free of Plog. "Our hands are just stuck together."

"Uh-huh," said Zill, as if this happened every day. "Well, I hope your butts aren't stuck to anything – because you need to shift them into the office right now." She pulled a face. "The All-Seeing PIE just had a funny turn."

Furp gasped.
"Our boss? A
funny turn?"

"I didn't know
computers
could turn at
all," said Plog.

"PIE is a
super-computer," Danjo reminded him.
"Perfect Intelligent Electronics,
remember? I bet he can do funny turns,
serious turns, many happy returns . . ."

"I mean, he just went really weird,"
Zill interrupted. "I was cleaning his
screen and polishing his wires. He was
talking away, and then he just sort of . . .
switched off."

"What?" Furp squealed in alarm.
"PIE never switches off – that's why he's
all-seeing. This could be serious . . ."
Twittering away, he went hopping at
high-speed along the tunnel to PIE's
office.

With a quick cough, Zill spat out a long rope of sticky slime at the ceiling, gripped it with her paws and swung all the way there in a couple of seconds like a bushy-tailed Tarzan.

"Wait for us!" yelled Danjo. As he ran after his teammates with Danjo, Plog found his heart was racing too. The All-Seeing PIE had brought the Slime Squad together to do good in Trashland – he was a mega-machine, created and then cast aside by Godfrey Gunk, the same human scientist who'd accidentally brought the rubbish dump to life. PIE had special sensors scattered far and wide throughout Trashland, and thanks to his 'Intelligent Electronics' he could use them like long-range eyes and ears.

Whenever these sensors detected danger, he sent the Slime Squad off to help.

But as Plog and Danjo burst into the vast human office through a door in the skirting-board, it seemed that PIE was the one who needed help. The computer's large, flickering screen suddenly flared neon bright as a million exclamation marks shone from within.

"Danger," groaned the super-computer. "Help! I am UNDER ATTACK!"

Chapter Two

TERROR IN OLD TOILET TRENCH

"Under attack?" Plog stared at PIE. "How can he be? There's no one in the room."

"ARRRGH!" PIE's hard-drive was whirring and squeaking as though stuffed with clockwork hamsters. "Poo . . . Disappearing poo . . ."

"He was saying the same thing before he went funny," said Zill.

"Sounds cool," said Danjo. "Poos that do magic tricks? Awesome."

15

"Be serious," said Zill. "PIE wasn't making it up – his sensors showed that all the rat and seagull poo had vanished from some of Trashland's smelliest cities."

"Danger . . ." PIE sounded delirious now. "Missing poo . . . poo . . ."

Furp clutched his crash helmet in fear. "I'm afraid he's gone poo-loopy. This calls for serious action!" The frog-monster started bounding about the computer's battered keyboard in a precise pattern, leaving slimy footprints on several keys. Suddenly, with a final electronic squeal, PIE's screen switched off completely.

Danjo's eyes almost popped out of his head. "You've killed him!"

"Not at all," Furp protested. "I've simply rebooted his system." With a fruity chime, PIE's workings began to whir and his screen started humming back to life. But would he be better or just like before? The Slime Squad held their breath. Plog found he was quite glad to be stuck with Danjo's hand to hold.

Finally, after what seemed an age, the screen became a reassuring slimy green colour. Two dots and a curly bracket appeared, shifting about to form PIE's familiar face. "Well," he boomed, "that wasn't much fun, I can tell you!"

17

"What happened?" asked Plog urgently.

"I'm not sure," rumbled the All-Seeing PIE. "I believe it was a long-range attack on my electronic mind."

Zill's tail was standing so far on end it almost brushed the ceiling. "But, you're a top-secret computer. No one knows you exist!"

"They must have discovered one of my remote sensors," said PIE slowly. "As you know, I am linked to each and every one. Those sensors allow me to look out over Trashland. But my mysterious attacker reversed that link and used it to look into *me*." He shuddered. "I've switched off that sensor now, but . . . they were using it to poke about in my databanks!"

"Why would anyone want to do that?" wondered Plog.

"Why wouldn't they, hmm?" PIE bristled. "I have very pretty databanks, stuffed full of the most gorgeous information."

Zill turned her worried bean-green eyes on Plog. "Perhaps some baddies want to take that info."

"But I don't understand," said Furp. "You and your sensors were built with human technology that we monsters barely understand ... so how could these baddies get at you so easily?"

"I don't know," PIE admitted. "But the sensor they used was hidden in Old Toilet Trench, which, as I was telling Zill, is one of the places which has become mysteriously poo-free." He paused.

"It's as if someone has gone out and gathered up every last smelly lump of the stuff."

"But who?" said Zill.

"I don't know," said PIE. "They must have done it extra-super-sneakily without me noticing. I'll just take a look through the sensor I keep at the other end of Old Toilet Trench. . . OW!" PIE suddenly broke off in electronic pain, and his screen changed colour to an alarming putrid pink. "Someone's tampering with *that* sensor too!"

Plog leaned forward, almost pulling Danjo off-balance. "Who, PIE?"

PIE began to shake as he brought the image of a deep furrow stuffed full of cracked, broken and half-buried old toilets up on his screen. For a moment, Plog glimpsed dark, shadowy shapes milling about in the pongy porcelain landscape . . .

Then a wisp of steam escaped PIE's casing and the picture disappeared. "ARRGH!" Exclamation marks began to fill his screen as before. "I'm under attack again! Must . . . resist . . ."

"Where exactly is this sensor, PIE?" Plog demanded. "If we race there in the Slime-mobile . . ."

"We can catch the attackers red-handed." Zill flashed her biggest grin at Plog. "Good thinking, Fur-boy."

"Yes, indeed," Furp twittered, studying the map that flashed up on PIE's flickering screen. "But we must hurry."

"Too right." Danjo raised a powerful pincer – lifting Plog off the floor as he did so. "'Cause when danger looms large, the Slime Squad cry—"

"CHARGE!" Plog shouted louder than anyone, leading the mad scramble back to the garage and into the Slime-mobile.

Zill grabbed her crime-fighting costume – a golden leotard – pulled it on while somersaulting through the air and landed with a bump in the driver's seat.

Plog and Danjo barely had a moment to grab hold of the two chairs behind her before she started the engine and pressed two paws onto the accelerator pedal.

"Full throttle mode!" Zill yelled. yanking down on the turbo-drive lever. The monster truck screeched away down the exit tunnel. Seconds later, a secret door opened up in the side of a

human builder's skip and they rocketed out. "I'll take a short cut through the Concrete Catacombs and Weed Forest." Furp ducked inside his lav-lab's slimy toilet and swapped his steel pants and crash helmet for identical golden versions.

But Plog and Danjo, still stuck together, found it trickier to change into their Slime Squad costumes — especially now they were being slung from side to side as Zill steered a mad, zigzag path through the traffic. Luckily, because the Slime-Mobile was invisible as well as astoundingly fast, no one else on the road even noticed.

Finally, just as Plog managed to pull a pair of golden shorts over his head — and as Danjo hid his crusty butt beneath a similar pair — Zill slowed down a little. "Old Toilet Trench is dead ahead."

Plog and Danjo looked through the windscreen at the grimy mountain landscape of chipped porcelain.

The pipes of giant upturned toilet pans poked out like periscopes. Rusty chains dangled from cracked cisterns like strange creepers.

And in the distance, Plog saw a group of strange blobby brown-and-silver figures of all shapes and sizes, gathered in the shadow of one toilet in particular.

Furp hopped forward to join the others at the windscreen, and gasped. "I do believe that's where PIE has his sensor. Those funny-looking things must be his attackers!"

"Then let's get them," Danjo scowled, "and make this mystery history."

Zill revved the engine and sent the Slime-mobile careering over the cracked porcelain at bone-juddering speed. As they neared the shadowy figures, she stamped on the brakes. Plog's heart was pounding like a box of electric clod-poppers as Furp tossed him a slime-shooter and passed another to Danjo.

"Thanks," said Danjo. "Now we can really stick it to these bad guys!"

Zill hit the door control and Plog and Danjo jumped outside, slime-shooters at the ready in their free hands. Zill galloped after them – while Furp jumped onto Danjo's back and pointed a stern finger. "Step away from that sensor," he warned the silent figures. "Or suffer the slimy consequences!"

One of the figures stirred in the shadows. "Intruders," it warned in a squelchy, hissing voice that sounded somehow mechanical. "Shall we retreat?"

"Negative," said a knobbly creature beside it, wearing funny headphones with a wire that disappeared deep inside the toilet. "We have not yet found the data we need."

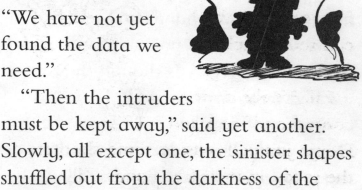

"Then the intruders must be kept away," said yet another. Slowly, all except one, the sinister shapes shuffled out from the darkness of the teetering toilet bowl to face the Slime Squad.

Plog gasped. Zill covered her mouth. Furp held his nose and Danjo stared in spooked-out wonder.

Impossible as it appeared, the threatening figures seemed to be made out of stinky, horrible poo! Some were dark and blobby like rat droppings. Others were streaked black and white as if made from birds' business. But each of the strange beasts had circuits and machinery pressed into their poopy bodies. Their eyes were like glowing bulbs. Their gooey mouths had rusty staples for teeth. Nails stuck out from their mucky hands and feet like claws. Wonky wires poked in and out of their smelly bodies, as though they were stitched through with steel.

"We are the Cyber-Poos," said the largest of the creepy creatures in that scary, squelchy voice. "You will leave this area at once – or be DESTROYED."

Chapter Three

THE POWER OF THE POOS

"We're not going anywhere." Trying to ignore the terrible smell, Plog set his face in a fierce scowl. "We don't care who you are or *poo* you are – you can't tell us what to do."

"Yes, I can," the creature informed him. "I am in control here. My name is Poo-Poo Prime." Ranged behind him, his muck-monster minions took a squashy step closer. "I repeat: you will leave this area at once."

"And I repeat, 'no.'" Plog tried to fold his arms — and poked himself in the ribs with Danjo's sticky claw. "We're here to stop you."

"Right," said Danjo. "So tell your poopy pals to stop messing with PIE's sensor and plop off."

Poo-Poo Prime's eyes glowed fierce red, and a metal nozzle slid out from his hand. "Stink pistol — activate!"

A haze of brown smelly gas sprayed from the nozzle. "Back!" Plog gasped to his teammates, clutching his throat — it felt on fire! His eyes ran and his nose almost fell off as the petrifying pong knocked him to his knees.

Danjo dragged Plog clear of the cloud and aimed his slime-shooter at Poo-Poo Prime.

"You asked for this," he growled, and
opened fire.

"Shield," said Poo-Poo Prime, his
circuits growing with an eerie brown
light. The 'stick-you' slime struck some
sort of invisible barrier around the
Cyber-Poo and sizzled to nothing in
moments.

"A matter-burning force-field!" Furp
spluttered. "That's incredible
technology."

Zill spat out a slime-strand to lasso a
poo – but its own shield activated and
her sticky rope went up in smoke.

Plog turned to his friends, his eyes still
streaming. "How can we stop them if
we can't touch them?"

"You CANNOT stop us," hissed Poo-Poo Prime, a nasty metal smile on his face. "All units – attack the Slime Squad!"

The Cyber-Poos lurched forwards, blobby hands outstretched to grab the four brave monsters.

"We can't fight all of them at once," Plog declared. "Split up!" As Furp and Zill darted away to the left, Plog and Danjo rolled away at ground level to the right.

"Here's an attack back atcha, my ploppy pals!" cried Danjo. He aimed his right pincer at the closest Cyber-Poo and let rip with a surge of sub-zero slime. Its shield flickered on at once, but Danjo kept pouring out the icy sludge until the entire creature was covered. "One down," he said proudly.

"Heating up circuits," hissed the smothered Cyber-Poo. And to Danjo's dismay, the slime-ice soon melted to nothing, revealing the muck-monster beneath to be utterly unharmed. It fired its stink pistol again and Danjo and Plog were driven back, choking even harder.

Two more Cyber-Poos closed in on Zill. She looked between them grimly. "Well, boys – if I can't touch you with my slime, I'll just have to touch you with something harder . . ." With that, she coughed out a slime-line that shot through the air and wrapped itself around the waste pipe of a toilet towering nearby. She tugged hard and the broken lav fell over, squashing the terrifying number twos. "Woo-hoo!" she cheered.

But Zill's happiness was short-lived as the toilet began to move. Straining their mucky muscles, the Cyber-Poos were actually lifting up the gigantic piece of porcelain. With a mechanical heave, they hurled it towards her! K-KRAAASHH! Zill barely twisted aside in time as the toilet hit the ground and started a shockwave that knocked her clean off her paws.

"These cyber-slop-bags have us at a disadvantage," Furp cried, trying to lead away Zill's attackers by hopping over their heads. "And every second we waste fighting them, the All-Seeing PIE is still under attack."

"Of course," Plog breathed as he and Danjo just barely dodged the dangerous claws of Poo-Poo Prime. "I know what we have to do!" He grabbed Danjo's slime-shooter and threw it to Furp. "Catch!"

Furp caught the weapon in mid-air and fired another jet of 'stick-you' slime at the menacing poo-monsters. But once again the spray sizzled up on their powerful shields.

"Don't fire at *them*," Plog shouted, and gestured instead towards the Cyber-Poo wearing headphones in the shadow of the toilet. "Fire at PIE's sensor so that horrible thing can't get to it!"

Furp beamed. "Brilliant!" Hopping higher than he had ever hopped before, the frog-monster hurtled past the lone Cyber-Poo and sloshed steaming slime into the dirty toilet bowl – sealing it completely.

"Yay!" cheered Zill. "You did it!"

But as Furp hopped quickly away, another Cyber-Poo pointed its fist at him. "Firing muck-missile," it growled – and a dollop of dung burst from its finger. The muck struck Furp on the bottom, and his round, metal pants erupted in a fierce explosion.

He dropped like a stone, crashing onto
the porcelain.

"Furp!" yelled Plog. He and Danjo
rushed forward to reach their friend
– but a looming Cyber-Poo stepped
forward to block their
way.

"Quick, Plog,"
Danjo shouted.
"Double-punch!"
His crusty claw
and Plog's furry
fist whooshed
through the air as
one and smashed the
Cyber-Poo aside before it could trigger
its shield. The monster thumped into the
invisible side of the Slime-Mobile and
slid slowly to the ground.

Danjo was shocked. "That one went
down like a dream."

"Lucky strike," Plog supposed. "Come
on!"

Zill got to Furp just ahead of them and checked him over. "I think he's just dazed," she said. "But we should get him back to the Slime-mobile."

Danjo looked up and gulped hard. "Um – actually, that might be kind of tricky."

With a sinking feeling, Plog saw Poo-Poo Prime approaching with his cyber-troops in a solid line, their revolting arms outstretched . . .

"Attention!" The Cyber-Poo with the headphones turned to his leader, red robotic eyes agleam. "The intruder's slime-attack came too late. I have taken the data we need."

"Excellent," hissed Poo-Poo Prime, halting his troops' advance. "Our master will be pleased with us."

"Master?" Plog sneered. "Let me guess
– you're being controlled by that stinky
mega-criminal Lord Klukk."

"We've taken him on before," said Zill.
"And won!"

But Poo-Poo Prime ignored them
both. "Come," he told his smelly soldiers.
"Now we have the information, phase
two of our plan must begin at once.
Return to HQ."

"Return to HQ," his troops repeated
in their horrid, squelchy voices. They
turned their backs on the Slime Squad
and made straight for the nearest
upturned toilet. Then they jumped down
inside, one after the other, landing
somewhere distantly
below with a
wet, sticky
splash.

"Farewell, slimy fools," rasped Poo-Poo Prime, his red eyes glowing. "But you will be seeing us again . . ." With that, he jumped down the enormous toilet and into the stinky unknown.

Plog, Zill and Danjo ran over to the poos' porcelain escape route. "I wonder where they've gone?" said Plog.

Furp sat up groggily. "There are sewers running beneath the ground here," he muttered. "They stretch from the Old Toilet Trench all the way to Silicon Ditch."

Zill peered down into the toilet bowl. Distantly, far below, she could hear a strange scraping sound. *Ker-scraaap . . . Ker-SCRAARRRP . . .* "The baddies' base must be down there somewhere," she mused.

"Maybe we should try to follow them?"

"Not now," said Plog. "Furp needs to rest, and we need to get back to the base and check that PIE's OK."

He and Danjo carried Furp aboard the Slime-mobile, and Zill started up the engines.

But as they departed the muddy china wilderness, none of them heard the sound of sinister, squelchy laughter from somewhere close by . . .

Chapter Four

TO SET A TRAP

Zill steered the Slime-mobile back through the wastelands to the secret base. All four Squaddies felt sore, cross and very worried.

Plog wiped his nose. "I keep thinking I can still smell those horrible monsters."

"Me too," said Zill.

Danjo sighed. "It's gonna take weeks to get the smell of old poos out of these shorts."

Zill parked the Slime-Mobile in its usual spot, and she, Furp, Plog and Danjo hopped out. Plog sniffed. The rank, rotten smell of poos was even stronger out here. He looked suspiciously at Danjo.

"Don't look at me," Danjo protested. "I went this morning before we left!"

The four friends raced away to the All-Seeing PIE's office.

"PIE!" Plog cried as he and Danjo burst through the door. "We know who attacked you – Cyber-Poos!"

Danjo nodded. "We just don't know where they came from or why they attacked you."

"We gummed up your sensor," said Furp. "But I'm afraid the Cyber-Poos had already taken the knowledge they needed."

"Yes, I know."
The dots of PIE's
eyes were spinning
about and his
mouth was a
downturned
bracket. "I tried to
stop my attackers
hacking into my
files . . . but they were
too strong. They stole my
most top-secret info — the hidden
locations of my two hundred all-seeing
sensors."

Plog gasped. "That means the Cyber-
Poos can find your sensors and break
them. You'll be the *Un*-seeing PIE!"

"Worse than that," Zill realized. "It
means that Poo-Poo Prime's master can
attack PIE from two hundred directions
at once."

"That could completely destroy me!"

A shocked silence fell across the office.

"Poo-Poo Prime said that phase poo – sorry, phase two – of their plan would begin at once," said Plog worriedly. "Whatever it is, we have to stop them."

"Easier said than done." Furp rubbed his sore bottom. "PIE, how come these Cyber-Poos and their master know so much about you?"

"I wonder . . ." said PIE. "No, that's ridiculous. He was destroyed . . . He can't be back."

"Who are you talking about?" Zill wondered, intrigued.

"Nobody," PIE snapped. "I don't believe in ghosts."

Plog looked puzzled. "What do ghosts have to do with anything?"

"Nothing. Nothing at all." PIE's screen turned pinky-red, almost as though he were blushing. "I don't know how these Cyber-Poos have learned how to attack me — but I DO know they have to be stopped."

"Maybe we could wipe them from the face of Trashland with a giant toilet roll," Danjo suggested.

"They'd only put up their shields, or blow it to bits or something," said Zill sadly. "They're just too strong for us."

"Especially with Plog and Danjo stuck together and unable to fight at full power." Furp sighed. "I really must find a way to unstick you both."

"First things first," said Plog. "PIE, it'll take the poos a long time to sabotage two hundred sensors.

Is there a quicker way of shutting you down?"

"I have a nasty feeling they will go straight for my Big Booster," said PIE, his voice wobbly. "It's hidden out in the Rubble Ruins and boosts power to all my remote parts – without it, my sensors wouldn't work at all."

"Sounds like a perfect target," said Zill.

"For us too." Furp's eyes opened wide. "If we know what the Cyber-Poos are after, we can get to the Rubble Ruins ahead of them and set an ambush!"

Danjo nodded with enthusiasm. "We could rig the rubble so it falls down on the Cyber-Poos when they come near."

Zill grinned. "And while they're busy dealing with that, we hit them with slime-shooters, slime-lines, hot slime, cold slime . . ."

"Everything!" Plog agreed, pointing down at his metal boots. "I'll even take these off and hit them with my super-smelly foot slime. I bet not even Poo-Poo Prime can cope with five attacks at once!"

"But just in case he can, let's hide the Big Booster somewhere else," said Zill. "That way it's safe, whatever happens."

PIE's screen showed a faint smiley face as he printed out a map showing the Big Booster's location. "Here you are," he murmured. "And . . . thank you for helping me. . ."

"You brought us together to protect innocent monsters from danger," Plog reminded him. "Now you're the one who needs protection."

"We'll sort out this mess," Danjo vowed. "You'll soon be an All-Seeing PIE again." And with Plog at his side, Danjo bombed off to the Slime-mobile, Furp and Zill close behind them.

Funny, thought Plog, *it still smells of poo around here. Maybe I got some up my nose?*

As the four brave monsters stormed on board their invisible vehicle, they didn't notice a squelchy figure watching them from the shadows of the underground garage, its eyes glowing an eerie green . . .

★

Within the hour, the Slime Squad were getting busy in the barren brickwork wilderness of the Rubble Ruins.

Furp soon found the Big Booster. It looked like a large cube of crystal with wires inside and was hidden halfway up a steep hill. He took it carefully and placed it on board the Slime-mobile, which was parked at the bottom of the slope. "There. Now if Poo-Poo Prime and his troops come after the Big Booster, they'll get a surprise."

"More than that," said Zill. She lingered halfway up the hill and started spitting out slime-lines, criss-crossing the different strands to make a slimy net.

"Old Toilet Trench and Silicon Ditch are to the south. So the Cyber-Poos will have to walk up this hill to find the Big Booster."

Plog nodded. "But instead they'll find your lovely net, filled with tons of rubble. And when they get close enough . . ."

"I burn through the side of the net with a blast of super-hot slime," Danjo broke in. "The rocks come crashing down the hillside—"

"And the poos get pelted," Zill concluded. "Hopefully it will weaken their shields enough for us to zap them with the slime-shooters."

Danjo and Plog, their hands still stuck

together, worked for the next hour filling the net with huge chunks of concrete while Zill kept watch for approaching Cyber-Poos.

"Almost finished," Plog panted, wiping his brow. "Hey, where's Furp? Why isn't he helping?"

"I can't," Furp called from the Slime-Mobile below. "I'm still working on a way to un-stick you and Danjo."

Danjo scowled. "I reckon he's just hiding from all the hard work."

"Ulp!" Zill's voice rose in pitch as she reared up onto her back legs and pointed to the top of the hill. "Hiding in the Slime-mobile sounds a good idea to me. Look!"

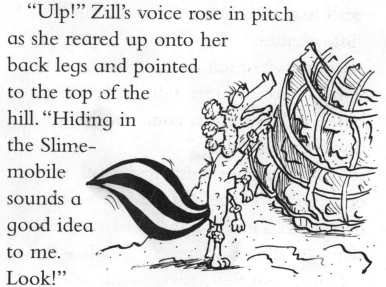

Plog turned as a huge, white shape flapped over the brow of the rubble-strewn hill, screeching as it settled on a hunk of concrete. Terror seized his insides: "It's a seagull!"

With their curved yellow beaks, wicked talons and appetite for monsters, the huge scavenging birds were feared throughout Trashland. But this particular seagull was the most frightening thing that Plog had ever seen — because perched on the bird's back was a knobbly, brown lump of niffy nastiness. The creature's cybernetic implants gleamed in the sunlight as it pointed a threatening nozzle down at the Slime Squad ... It was a Cyber-Poo!

Chapter Five

THE BEST SLAYED PLANS

"Oh, fabulous," Danjo groaned. "Those poop-brained ploppers were meant to come to the bottom of this hill so we could get them – not come over the top of it on seagulls!"

Plog gulped as another five Cyber-Poos trudged stickily over the brow of the hill. *They must've sneaked round the back*, he realized, as the creatures raised their stink pistols, ready to fire.

Zill might just dodge an attack, but Danjo and I make too big a target.

"We know of your plans to ambush us," rasped the Cyber-Poo perched on the seagull's back. "Our spy sneaked into your secret base by clinging to the bottom of the Slime-mobile."

"I guess poos and bottoms go well together," said Danjo sourly.

Plog looked at Zill. "No wonder we smelled something."

"The spy magnetized his metal parts so he could not fall off," explained the proud poo-monster. "Just as I have magnetized my own metal bits so I can cling to the iron ring I have placed around this bird. By transmitting high-pitched stink-o-waves into its brain I can steer it anywhere."

"That's, like, totally interesting." Plog pretended to yawn. "Why not steer it somewhere else, before you bore us all to death?"

"I can't believe we let one of those things get inside our base." Zill groaned. "We left poor PIE defenceless!"

The seagull lowered its head and the Cyber-Poo laughed nastily. "Hand over the Big Booster now and perhaps we shall spare him."

Plog turned helplessly to the Slime-Mobile. "Furp!" he called. "You'd better do as the big poo says."

"What?" Furp's muffled voice carried

from the Slime-mobile. "Oh, dear, dear, dear. Yes, I suppose I must give our smelly friend what he desires . . ." The chemistry genius came outside. In his hands he clutched a transparent cube, shining in the sunlight.

"Bring it to us," grated the Cyber-Poo.

Using his slime-coated foot-soles to stick to the rubble, Furp swiftly scaled the slope. He paused beside Plog, Danjo and Zill. Plog looked at him sadly, and Furp shrugged. Rather than climb the rest of the way, he tossed the cube to the evil number two, who caught it in both hands.

"Thank you." He hissed with smelly satisfaction and passed the object to a fellow poo, who popped it into a ragged cardboard box for protection. "Very soon now, our master's plans will be complete. But first . . ." He turned to his poopy posse. "ELIMINATE THE SLIME SQUAD!"

A hail of brown, squidgy missiles shot from a dozen stinky fingers.

"Zill, Furp – down!" yelled Plog, diving with Danjo behind the slime-net full of concrete.

"Um, actually, that might not be such a good idea," Furp twittered, as one of Zill's slimy strands sizzled and sagged under the weight of so much rubble. "I rather think the Cyber-Poos are firing at the net . . ."

59

Zill gasped as she realized what their enemies were up to. "They're going to crush us with our own booby-trap!"

"Quickly – run!" Plog heaved Danjo after him, stumbling down the steep concrete hillside as it started to shake. "We must reach the Slime-mobile before we're buried alive!"

Furp jumped past them, dodging deadly poo-splats as he went. Zill spat out another slime line and swung down the hillside.

Ka-ka-KA-KA-KROOOOOM! The slime net gave way behind them, and massive chunks of rock and rubble began bouncing down the hill after the four desperate superheroes.

"Keep going!" Plog shouted, clinging onto Danjo for dear life as they hurled themselves inside the Slime-mobile and slammed into the far wall. The whole vehicle rocked violently. Furp jumped in after them and landed straight in the lav-lab's toilet while Zill swung herself into the driver's seat and hit the engines.

The roar of falling rubble was building to a grating, stone-crunching screech.

"Get us out of here, Zill!" Plog shouted.

"On the case, Fur-boy." Zill stamped on the accelerator and the Slime-mobile sped away just as the first chunks of concrete hammered down around them. A few seconds later and the bottom of the hill was buried under stacks of stone.

"Thank goodness for that," said Furp, only his feet visible, sticking out of the toilet. "We made it."

"Don't speak too soon." Zill was looking grimly in the rear-view mirror. "That Cyber-Poo and his gull are coming after us!"

Plog saw that she was right – a menacing white-and-brown shape was whooshing out of the sky towards them. With a deep, laughing cry the zombie seagull drew closer. The Cyber-Poo astride it fired a volley of brown bombs down at the Slime-mobile.

"These poos are bad news," said

Danjo. "Can we outrun them?"

The Slime-mobile shook with the force of a ploppy explosion. "I guess not," Plog muttered.

"We have one chance," said Furp, struggling out of the lav-lab's lavvy. "The Cyber-Poo said he was controlling the seagull with high-pitched stink-o-waves." He grabbed a screwdriver from his pants, pulled off his crash helmet and started jabbing at the radar dish that crowned it. "If I can use this to transmit stink-o-waves, I might be able to jam the poo's commands . . ."

Outside, the seagull swooped low overhead, and Zill swung the Slime-mobile from side to side as the Cyber-Poo launched more messy missiles. "You said 'might'," she yelled. "Aren't you sure?"

"Not remotely," Furp admitted. Then he rounded on Plog. "Quickly, take off your boots!"

Plog frowned down at the water-filled cauldrons he wore on his tootsies. "But you know what will happen – out of liquid and into fresh air, my feet start oozing horrible slime."

"Precisely, my dear Plog." The Slime-mobile rocked again as a muck missile dented the roof, and Furp almost dropped his screwdriver.

"Horrible and very, very smelly slime. If I dip my helmet in that toxic goo, it should put real stink into my stink-o-waves!"

Plog was already pulling his boots off.

He closed his eyes
and braced himself
for the worst – and
his feet really *were* the
worst. Within seconds,
bright yellow, gruesome
goo began to drip from his toes.

"Ugh!" Danjo put his free pincer to
his nose. "This is one time when being
stuck to you really stinks!"

"Don't knock it," said Furp. "We know
Plog's slime has a hundred-and-one
household uses." He dipped his helmet in
the evil-smelling foot sauce. "Let's just
hope it has a hundred-and-two!"

Plog stared at the silent helmet.
"Nothing's happening," he cried.

Another muck-missile rocketed into its
target. Zill struggled with the steering
wheel as the Slime-mobile was almost
blown off the road. "Quickly!" she
shouted. "We can't take much more
of this . . ."

But suddenly the sticky radar dish
started spinning round, super-fast. Furp
beamed. "I . . . I think it's starting to
work!" As the seagull swooped closer to
deliver another deadly bombardment, he
jammed the screwdriver into the
helmet's workings. A warbling whine
went up . . .

And the seagull suddenly squawked
furiously and veered away. The
Cyber-Poo gave an electronic gurgle
as the bird broke for freedom,
soaring higher and higher
into the air. "Out of
control," he yelled, his
voice growing fainter.
"All units, assistance
required. Help . . .
Help . . . !"

"It worked!"
Zill cheered.

Plog felt
dizzy with

relief as he pulled on his metal boots
again, drowning his slime in the warm
water inside. "Furp, you're a genius."
"True!" Furp switched off his
helmet. "But I couldn't have
done it without your feet."
"Unfortunately!" Danjo
wiped whiffy foot slime
from his face. "But
what about PIE? We left
him alone with a Cyber-
Poo in the base – and
we've given those stink-heads
his Big Booster."
"Actually, we haven't."
Furp reached into the
lav-lab's
lav with a
knowing smile . . .
and pulled out a
glass box with
wires inside.
"Ta-daaa!"

"The Big Booster – it's still here!" Zill frowned. "Then . . . what did you give the Cyber-Poos?"

"A chunk of Danjo's slime ice!" Furp explained. "I had a big cube in the freezer. It's one of the ingredients in the serum I'm making to un-stick him and Plog."

"Never mind us," said Danjo. "It's PIE I'm worried about. If those things have hurt him, the Big Booster won't matter in any case."

Plog nodded miserably. "Without PIE, the Slime Squad is finished – and the way will be clear for evil monsters to take over our world!"

Chapter Six

WHERE'S THE LAIR?

Zill pressed the pedal to the metal,
speeding all the way back to the base. But
as the Slime-Mobile neared the human
house that hid their HQ, she brought it
screeching to a stop. "Oh, no . . ."

Plog charged forward with Danjo and
Furp to see what Zill was staring at
through the windscreen. Butterflies filled
his stomach as he saw the
cellar window was
smashed to
pieces — with a
large, computer-
sized hole in the
pane.

"I . . . I don't believe it." Furp flung open the Slime-Mobile doors and hopped outside, right up onto the windowsill. "The office is empty. You know what this means, don't you?" He swung round to face his friends, fear in his froggy eyes. "Cyber-Poos have kidnapped the All-Seeing PIE!"

Plog, Danjo and Zill joined Furp outside. The entire area was splashed with bird droppings.

"The Cyber-Poos must've ridden here on their seagulls," Danjo noted. "Loads of them by the look of things."

"Once they knew where PIE was,

they attacked in force," Zill agreed.

Plog nodded. "But how did they get him outside?"

Furp picked up a scrap of red rubber caught on one of the jagged bits of glass left in the window frame, then bounced down to rejoin the Squad. "I believe this was once a balloon." He licked the inside with his long tongue and pulled a face. "A helium balloon, unless I'm very much mistaken – a balloon that floats. I bet the poos tied lots of balloons to PIE to lift him into the air and then used their pet seagulls to tow him away!"

Plog brightened. "Then the Cyber-Poos haven't killed PIE – they've taken him prisoner. And that means we can break him out!"

"But how?" Zill gestured around.

"They could have taken him anywhere – there are no tracks to follow."

"No tracks in the ground, anyway," said Furp, a sly gleam in his eye. "But we know that the Cyber-Poos control their seagulls with stink-o-waves. And my helmet is now tuned into those smelly signals." He pulled his screwdriver from his pants and started to tinker. "With a tweak or two, I'm sure I can track them to their source – the lair of the Cyber-Poos." Plog shivered. "How scary is that?"

"To stand a chance of success, we must all be at the peak of our powers." Furp hopped back inside the lav-lab and set down his helmet on the toilet.

"So, while my radar dish pinpoints the source of the stink-o-waves, let's see if I can un-stick you and Danjo." He picked up a beaker of bright orange liquid. "I'm certain that this mixture of Zill's spittle and Danjo's pincer-slush will free you both from my 'stick-you' slime." He paused. "Well, fairly certain . . . ish." He paused again. "Look, it might work without exploding – shall we give it a try?"

Danjo and Plog looked at each other and sighed. Then they nodded.

"Here goes nothing!" Furp poured the orange goo onto his friends' gummed-up hands, and the slimy substance began to steam and sizzle. "Now, quickly. Pull, the pair of you!"

Plog and Danjo strained to free themselves. The sticky gunk stretched like extra-gooey cheese on a slimy pizza. "It's working," Plog gasped, staggering backwards while Danjo heaved in the other direction. "The glue's weakening . . . it's not so sticky . . ."

But then suddenly – "Oooof!" Plog and Danjo were catapulted back into each other and fell sprawling to the dirty floor.

"Oh." Furp frowned. "It seems my new goo *does* make the 'stick-you' slime a little less sticky . . . But not for very long."

Zill couldn't help but smile.

"I think they noticed!"

But suddenly the radar dish on Furp's helmet started to spin and smoke. A foul pong filled the Slime-mobile.

"Ugh!" Danjo choked. "That whiff's almost as bad as Plog's feet!"

"It means my 'stink-o-wave picker-upper' is working!" Furp bounced around in mad excitement, dragging wires and cables from out of an old smelly-vision set and connecting them to the helmet. A grainy image appeared on the screen – piles and piles of computer parts and circuit boards stretching into the distance. "The signals are coming from somewhere underneath that lot."

"Silicon Ditch!" Zill exclaimed. "Not very far from Old Toilet Trench."

"PIE told us that poos had gone missing from that area," Plog recalled.

"And I bet the sewers at Old Toilet Trench run under Silicon Ditch too," said Danjo. "That's why the plop-heads jumped down the toilet when they pushed off before."

"It's time we were pushing off ourselves." Plog clenched his fists and looked around at his friends. "We've got a super-computer to save!"

As Zill drove the Slime-mobile closer to Silicon Ditch, the radar dish spun faster and faster. Furp hopped between the screen and the crash-helmet, scribbling down stink-o-wave calculations.

"I've managed to pinpoint the exact location of the Cyber-Poos' base," he announced at last, placing the helmet back on his head. "It's very close by."

"You'd better stop the Slime-mobile, Zill," Plog called. "We'll investigate on foot."

"Good." Zill braked, jumped up and opened the doors. "I've had quite enough of driving for one day."

Plog stared out onto a high-tech landscape of cracked circuit boards, broken fuses and squashed silicon chips. There were no monsters in sight, no seagulls and certainly no poos. Beyond Silicon Ditch he could see the vast stretch of rusting human gadgets that formed the Heavy Metal Hills. A huge crane-like vehicle stood at the border between the two territories, dangling a gigantic metal disc.

"What's that thing?" Plog asked Furp. "The Cyber-Poos' sentry?"

"No. It's just an old human machine," Furp explained. "That steel disc is actually a massive electromagnet – a magnet that works off electricity. Whenever human giants wanted to shift a pile of metal scrap they simply switched on the magnet to pick up the stuff and switched the magnet off again when they were ready to drop it. As a matter of fact, monster landscape experts believe that's how the Heavy Metal Hills were formed . . ."

Zill yawned. "I'm like an electromagnet – I just switched off too."

"Yeah," Danjo added, "thanks for the geography lesson, Furp, but we've got bigger fish to fry with our silicon chips.

There must be a PIE-sized secret entrance somewhere, leading to the underground base."

"Perhaps the Poos use the electromagnet to open a hidden metal hatch or something," Furp suggested.

"But how will we find a way in?" Plog wondered. He jumped down, pulling Danjo after him.

CRACK! went the ground beneath them.

"Uh-oh . . ." Danjo swapped a helpless look with Plog. "Whoaaaaaaa!"

With a snapping of circuit boards, the ground gave way beneath Plog and Danjo's feet and they fell through empty space into deep, cold blackness . . .

Chapter Seven

TO SMELL AND BACK

"*Arrrrrrrrgh!*"

Zill and Furp heard Plog and Danjo cry out as they fell through the ground – and then land heavily with a THUMP!

"Great jumping slimeballs!" Furp gasped. "I do believe they've found a way in." He stared down at what seemed to be a length of plastic drainpipe disappearing down into the darkness.

"Hmm, most likely an air-vent. Even Cyber-Poos can't breathe their own smell all day."

"We've got to get down there and see if they're all right," said Zill. She spat out a slime-line, bit through it, slammed one end in the Slime-Mobile's doors and quickly climbed down the sticky strand into the darkness. Furp followed, using his slimy hands and feet to crawl down the drainpipe like a froggy spider.

Zill crept out cautiously into a cold concrete cavern — part of the system of sewer pipes built beneath Trashland. It stank of old poos, and was lit with a spooky brown glow.

Plog and Danjo were a short distance away, standing at a T-junction in the pipe work, peering into the gloom. "Hey!" she hissed. "Are you two all right?"

"We're great!" Danjo ran back to her – and for once, Plog wasn't pulled along behind. "Furp's new goo must've weakened the 'stick you' slime – and the fall finally bumped us free!"

"Thank goodness," said Furp, hopping out of the pipe. "If we're going to fight an entire lair full of savage Cyber-Poos, we'll need every advantage we can get."

Plog suddenly stiffened. "I think there's something else down here," he said hoarsely. "Listen!"

Sure enough, a spooky scraping sound was cutting through the cold air – *ker-SCRARPP! Ker-SCRARRRRRP!*

"It's the same noise I heard floating up from beneath Old Toilet Trench," Zill realised.

"Get back!" Plog turned and shooed his friends back into the shadows. "Whatever it is, it's coming this way!"

The Slime Squad held their breaths as the raggedy scraping sound got louder and a strange shadow fell across the far wall of the tunnel. Plog almost gasped out loud as a weird, menacing monstrosity came into sight.

It was a thing of muck and metal, shaped like an enormous sideways 'V' – although its hard steel lines were softened with splats of dung. Plog saw that it had the remains of a keyboard on its lower half and a broken screen on its top half – and was dragging itself forward on odd mechanical attachments. Poo-Poo Prime and four Cyber-Poo bodyguards squelched along just behind it.

Zill stared in shock as the huge, metal thing crept past. "It's . . . like a portable PIE!"

"Looks more like a poo-poo pie to me," Danjo muttered. "It's dented, it's dirty . . . But it's got to be the master of these Cyber-Poos, right?"

Furp nodded fearfully. "It's a human invention," he whispered. "A special kind of computer called a laptop. But I've never heard of one being able to move all by itself."

"It looks as though PIE isn't the only super-computer in Trashland," breathed Plog. "And maybe, just maybe, this laptop thing doesn't like the competition." As the scraping and squelching began to fade, Plog stepped out of hiding. "Come on. We'd better follow that pooper-computer – we might overhear where it's keeping PIE."

The four Squaddies stayed close and stuck to the shadows, edging after the mobile laptop through toxic-smelling tunnels littered with muck and electronic parts. Down one passageway, Plog saw what looked like an enormous egg-box connected to a thick wire. It glowed yellow, and oozed thick brown sludge.

Then the lid of the egg box flipped open to reveal six Cyber-Poos inside, their metal implants shining in the sinister light.

"So that's how ordinary droppings taken from up above are turned into computerized Cyber-Poos," Plog realized with a shiver. "And more and more of the horrible things are being made. But why?"

Then a familiar voice echoed distantly along the tunnel and Plog's heart leaped. "How dare you keep me locked up like this?"

Zill clutched hold of Plog's arm in excitement. "That sounds like PIE!"

Danjo nodded. "He must be somewhere up ahead."

"But that living laptop is between us and him," Furp said nervously.

"I demand to talk to whoever's in charge," PIE went on. "At once."

As the Squaddies crept round a corner in the sewer tunnel and peered past the laptop, they could see their electronic friend. He'd been dumped in a puddle and was guarded by at least twenty Cyber-Poos. Popped balloons and bits of string were draped all around him. And as the stinky laptop approached, massive exclamation marks appeared on PIE's screen. "No . . . it can't be you . . ."

"But it IS me!" the laptop rasped, his voice hissing and gurgling. "Your 'old friend' from the human world – the Sophisticated Mega-Electronic Living Laptop."

Furp blinked in the shadows. "Or 'SMELL' for short."

"No wonder you knew how to get into my databanks," PIE realized. "You were built by Godfrey Gunk, just as I was, using the same technology." He paused, his screen flashing a shock of bright colours. "But you stopped working ages ago. Your circuits overloaded, so Godfrey threw you away."

"Yes, he did," the laptop growled. "Once, I was shiny and new – his greatest creation. But after a while, I wasn't enough for him. So Godfrey built you – made you better and smarter and self-repairing. You became the apple of his PIE . . . while I just hung around like an old SMELL."

"No machine lasts for ever," said PIE gently. "Before he left, Godfrey tried to trash me too. He didn't want anyone else to use his technology."

"Well, he trashed me good and proper!" The laptop hissed angrily. "Then he chucked me into a sewer in the far corner of the dump. I ended up buried under all sorts of horrible muck. But one day, radiation kick-started my circuits and pumped power into the plops that covered me ..."

"And brought you back as a com-POO-ter," said PIE sadly. "But you never used to be a bad SMELL. It's the muck inside you that's turned you evil. Why have you made these terrible Cyber-Poos?"

"We are SMELL's servants," gurgled Poo-Poo Prime.

"They will help me gain power over all Trashland," SMELL revealed. "And so will you, my dear 'old friend'. So will you . . ."

"No!" PIE rocked crossly from side to side, his screen darkening. "Never!"

"We shall see." *Ker-SCRAAPE. Ker-SCRAAAAAP.* Shuffling forwards, chuckling evilly, SMELL and his Cyber-Poos closed in on the helpless PIE . . .

Chapter Eight
BROWN ALERT

With PIE in danger, Plog braced himself to burst out and lead the Slime Squad into action.

But suddenly, a big BEEP burst from SMELL's casing. "Curses," the com-poo-ter rasped. "I must take this call."

With a loud *ker-SCRAAAPE* he turned on the spot until he was facing the Slime Squad, who cringed even deeper into the sewer shadows.

Plog frowned as a
familiar silhouette
appeared on
SMELL's poop-
splashed screen
– the shadow of a
large, chicken-like
creature with a
curved, cruel beak and a sinister wobbly
bit on top of its head.

"Lord Klukk," breathed Plog. "So that
bird-brained monster is behind all this."

"Well?" SMELL's eyes turned inwards
to his screen. "What do you want,
Klukk?"

"That's Lord Klukk to you," squawked
the shadow. "How dare you disrespect
me! It was I who dug you out from the
poop that held you . . . I who gave you
this secret *buk-buk*-base. I who supplied
you with the dung you needed to make
an army of Cyber-Poos. Without me,
you would be nothing."

"And without my superior – or should I say, *poo*-perior – technology, you can't get the power you crave over Trashland," SMELL retorted. "That's the only reason you've helped me, and we both know it!"

"Enough," Klukk hissed. "Have you set up my all-seeing spy network yet?"

"The matter is in hand," SMELL said airily. "When the network is complete, you will be able to see anywhere in Trashland from the comfort of your evil lair. You'll have the power to spy on any monster, anywhere in the land, twenty-four hours a day."

"Ah, good." Lord Klukk clucked with pleasure. "Very good . . ."

Plog gasped. "So that's what this is all about. Klukk doesn't want to destroy PIE's powers . . ."

"He wants them for himself!" Furp concluded.

"Soon, the Cyber-Poos will take over Trashland," Klukk hissed. "Should any monsters try to fight *buk-buk*-back, I will spot them on the spy-network and alert my mucky minions. All resistance will be crushed." He sniggered nastily, his sinister squawk rising to a shriek. "I shall rule over everyone. King of the world! Nothing will *buk-buk*-be able to stand in my way. NOTHING!"

With a gurgling snort, SMELL cut across Klukk's mad mutterings. "I think you're forgetting, I am to be the ruler of Silicon Ditch and the Poo-nited States of Trashland."

"Eh? What?" Klukk settled back down.

"Er, yes, of course. That will *buk-buk*-be your reward for serving me well."

"Quite," said SMELL. "So the sooner you stop gassing on and let me get on with things, the better."

"Just do not fail me, you leaky old *lav*-top," Klukk warned him. "Or else!" His shadow faded from the screen.

"So Lord Klukk knows all about me now, does he?" said PIE quietly.

"No." SMELL scraped himself back round to face the imprisoned computer. "I have kept your existence secret – in case he tried to deal directly with you instead of with me. I needed his support and supplies to build my Cyber-Poo forces."

"So Klukk can't know where our secret base is hidden," Zill whispered.

"That's something!"

"But, really, SMELL," boomed PIE. "You can't believe that Lord Klukk will keep his word and let you rule part of Trashland?"

"Of course not," growled the com-poo-ter. "He will try to trick me. But only I control the Cyber-Poos."

Poo-Poo Prime nodded his lumpy head. "We will strike first – wiping out Lord Klukk and his followers."

SMELL laughed, a grating, electronic roar. "And when I have taken control of your scattered circuits and sensors, PIE, I will become the All-Seeing SMELL. Trashland will be mine! I shall force all living monsters to build more and more Cyber-Poos. They will build me an army big enough to

96

invade the human world, hunt down
Godfrey Gunk and make him pay for
what he did to me!"

PIE almost toppled over in shock.
"You must be potty as well as pooey,"
he declared. "But your plan won't work.
My sensors are useless to you without
the Big Booster." He looked past
SMELL and into the
shadows, as
though he knew
the Slime
Squad hid
there. "And my
team would
destroy it rather
than let it fall into enemy hands."

"Those slimy fools may have escaped
my seagull sentries for now," SMELL
rasped. "But soon they will be captured,
and the Big Booster will be mine."

"No way," Plog murmured. He turned
to his friends and nodded towards the

way they had come. "You heard PIE.
We must get back to the Slime-mobile,
blitz the Big Booster and then think up
a way to save PIE. Come on!"

Plog led Zill, Furp and Danjo back
along the tunnel towards the air vent. As
he passed the mucky, mechanical egg-
box he'd seen earlier, he saw that it was
empty . . .

And then realized six fresh Cyber-
Poos were blocking the way ahead!

"Alert," grated one of the monsters.
"Alert. ALERT."

Brown flashing lights went off all
around them, and a siren started up.

"Oh, great!" Danjo fired a blast of
red-hot slime from his left pincer – but

the creatures threw up their shields and the goo sizzled harmlessly to nothing. "Man, those poos are fast!"

"Intruders? Here?" SMELL's eyes narrowed as he turned quickly to see. "Who would dare?"

Poo-Poo Prime's circuits buzzed. "Intruders identified as the Slime Squad."

"Catch them!" boomed SMELL. "They have the Big Booster. Catch them at all costs!"

The six Cyber-Poos blocking the Squad's way shuffled forwards, their weapons extending . . .

Chapter Nine

FOUR AGAINST AN ARMY

"Furp," snapped Plog as the Cyber-Poos lumbered closer. "Hop to it!"

Furp leaped clear over the Cyber-Poos' heads. As the six pongy plop-monsters turned to fire muck missiles in his direction, Zill spat out a slime-line and caught them by surprise, wrapping two of the creatures together. At the

same time, Danjo flattened them with a
power-packed pincer-punch.

"Charge!" Plog commanded, racing
through the gap in the monsters' ranks.
Danjo and Zill sped after him.

Soon they reached Furp, who was
waiting at the bottom
of the pipe that led
back up to the
surface. "Quickly!" he
urged his friends.
"Those Cyber-Poos
must be hopping
mad."

"Plopping mad,
more like," said
Danjo, rushing to join
him. Looking up he
could see a distant
patch of sky at the
top of the pipe. "Plog,
we'd better get
climbing."

"See you at the top, guys." Zill spat out a super-long slime strand that stuck to the very top of the pipe. Sucking it back into her mouth like spaghetti, she pulled herself up while Danjo dug his many pincers into the plastic sides and climbed like a crimson mountaineer. Plog followed on in the hand-and-footholds the crab-creature left behind, clinging on for dear life.

Within seconds, Poo-Poo Prime had reached the bottom of the pipe with the Cyber-Poo bodyguards.

"Offensive action – activate!"

The misshapen dung-devils fired up at Plog and Danjo. The pipe filled with muck missiles and evil clouds of stink spray but the squaddies kept on climbing. As they reached the top, Zill and Furp helped them scramble out onto the high-tech wasteland of Silicon Ditch.

"Made it," Plog grunted.

Zill beamed at him. "Those stink-heads will have a tough time following us now!"

But suddenly, the ground began to shake and old monitors toppled over with a crash as a huge zigzagging split opened up lengthways along Silicon Ditch, dividing it in two. Each side slowly slid back to reveal a gaping hole in the circuit-strewn surface – and moments later, Cyber-Poos on seagulls burst out from inside the split, soaring into the air!

"So much for them using giant electromagnets to open a secret hatch every time they want to get in and out," Danjo groaned. "The entrance is automatic. We're really for it now!"

"I underestimated SMELL's technology," Furp admitted. "Clearly they got PIE into their base by lowering him down through there."

"Never mind that now," said Plog. "Come on!" He led the charge to the Slime-mobile, but a wave of brown bombs hit the ground just ahead of them. The fierce heat and smell drove the four monster heroes backwards.

"Surrender!" droned the flying poos, gliding overhead. "Surrender!" Danjo dived for cover as muck missiles went off nearby and pongy poop fragments flew through the air.

"Actually they're pretty rubbish shots, aren't they?"

"They're shooting to scare us," Plog realized. "They can't fire right at us in case they blow up the Big Booster."

"But they're stopping us from reaching the Slime-mobile," Zill yelled over another explosion.

"Furp," Plog shouted. "Can you scramble the Cyber-Poos' stink-o-wave signals again, so they can't control their birds?"

"It would be a pleasure," Furp assured him, already fiddling with his crash helmet. The radar dish began spinning backwards and the gulls shrieked and hooted, shaking their filthy jockeys from their stained brown backs. CLANG! SPLAT! The Cyber-Poos plummeted earthward – but soon got back up again and joined their fellows, advancing on the Slime Squad.

"Attack," they rasped. "Eliminate. Destroy."

With the aerial attack over, Plog ran to the Slime-mobile and threw open the doors. "All aboard – now!'

But as the Squaddies ran inside they saw a large red helium balloon float out from the Cyber-Poos' base – with SMELL himself dangling underneath, his dung-covered casing clamped round the balloon's neck tightly. Poo-Poo Prime was perched on his master's lid.

As the balloon drifted over solid ground, the laptop let go and landed with an eerie rattle. "Release poison-parp grenades," SMELL commanded. "Maximum strength – whiffy enough to kill!"

"We obey," hissed Poo-Poo Prime. "All units – full-strength stink-out. Activate!"

With a menacing whirring noise, steel tubes rose out of the Cyber-Poos' heads and launched small brown balls into the air. Zill slammed the Slime-Mobile doors. The  deadly parp grenades went off outside with a very rude noise.

"Oh, my giddy gonkberry!" gasped Furp, pointing to wisps of smoke curling through the tiniest of gaps in the doors:

"Deadly bottom gas is getting in!"

Danjo raised his cold pincer and squirted icy slime over the whole area, sealing the doors solid. "There! Now we can zoom away from here."

"But even if we do, and even if we destroy the Big Booster, PIE's still their prisoner." Plog felt like tearing his fur out. "We'll never get him away from that evil lair, and the Cyber-Poos will still attack Trashland. What are we going to do?"

"The electromagnet!" Furp cried suddenly.

Danjo frowned. "Will you shut up about the electromagnet?"

"Drive us there, Zill," Furp urged her. "It's our only chance."

"Better do as he says, Zill." The Slime-mobile rocked as a muck missile smashed through the rear windscreen and whizzed past Plog's long ears. "Let her rip."

"You got it!" Zill accelerated away towards the Heavy Metal Hills and the giant electromagnet that stood before it.

"Pursue the Slime Squad!" SMELL shrieked. "Catch them. CRUSH them!"

Plog turned to Furp desperately as the Slime-Mobile rocked and rattled away. "What's your plan?"

"We know these creatures' metal parts are magnetic," said Furp. "That's how they stuck to the seagulls' saddles, and how their Cyber-Spy clung to the underside of this very vehicle. So if we can lure them into the electromagnet's range . . ."

"They'll be hoisted up by their metal bits and left dangling miles above us." Danjo smiled. "Sweet plan."

"Except they all have cyber-shields," Zill reminded them. "Those things might protect them from the magnet's power."

"That's if the old wreck works at all," added Danjo, looking worried. "It hasn't been used in years. It won't have any power."

"You're good with electrics, Danjo," said Furp. "You must get it working. And Zill, you can steer any vehicle – including that crane, yes?"

"But that's a human-giant vehicle," she protested. "It won't be easy."

111

"Staying alive won't be easy, either,"
said Plog grimly, pointing through the
shattered rear window. "Look!"

It seemed that every single Cyber-Poo
was chasing after them, squelching at
super-speed across a sea of old circuits.
Zill pushed the Slime-Mobile's engines
to their limit, but their pursuers were
clearly powering their mechanical parts
to the max too. Even SMELL was
scraping his way towards them with
uncanny speed.

"We're not going to make it," groaned
Danjo. "We've done our best – but this
looks like Game Over!"

Chapter Ten

THE FINAL STINK-OUT

"Stop the Slime-Mobile, Zill," Plog shouted, and as she hit the brakes, he grabbed a slime-shooter from a bench. "I'll jump out and distract them to buy you more time."

"Me too," said Furp, hefting another slime-shooter.

"But you'll both be killed!" Zill protested.

"Maybe not," Furp muttered, grabbing an orange beaker and pouring it into his rifle.

"Hmm. Yes, it might just work . . ."

"Eh?" said Danjo. "What do you—?"

"No time for talk," Furp told him, pouring the orange stuff into Plog's slime-shooter too. "You and Zill must GO!"

With that, he and Plog dived through the shattered rear window and landed on a bed of broken circuits. Zill and Danjo drove on in the Slime-Mobile, heading for the electromagnet as SMELL and the Cyber-Poos kept up their grisly advance.

"Let's blast these dirty devils, Furp." Plog shot a big slimy stream at the onrushing tide of semi-robotic muck. As usual, it sizzled away on their super-strength shields.

"No, no, my dear Plog," said Furp.

"Fire over the ground in front of us. Soak it silly!"

"'Silly' is right." Plog ducked as the poos fired yet more muck missiles. "What's the point of spraying the ground? Your 'stick you' slime is super-quick-drying, remember?"

"But I've just added in my attempt at an antidote!" Furp cried. "Remember when I tried to unstick you and Danjo? It makes my super-duper slime-glue softer and less sticky – but not for very long."

"Of course!" Plog nodded. "A few seconds later, the slime goes back to being super-sticky – but hopefully it will stay soft long enough for the Cyber-Poos to trample through it with shields off."

115

"With luck, they won't realize the ground's getting stickier and stickier," Furp agreed. "Until it's too late!"

The Cyber-Poos kept on coming, shooting their sprays and missiles. Plog opened fire at ground level, backing away towards the crane as he went, and Furp did just the same.

"Squish them!" snarled Poo-Poo Prime.

"Squelch them!" SMELL yelled.

"Keep squirting, Furp!" cried Plog.

★

"Made it!" Zill shouted. With the Slime-mobile's doors still iced up, she and Danjo scrambled out through the broken back window.

The colossal crane with its electromagnet loomed overhead. Zill spat a slime-line up at the huge steel disc and swung up into the dusty driver's cab with Danjo hanging onto her back paws. Once inside, she spun slime lines over the controls, pulling on different strands to try and get the magnet working. "You were right, Danjo," she wailed. "No power!"

"We'll see about that," puffed Danjo, his pincers tearing through wires and

workings. He pushed
two bare wires
together and the
engine spluttered into life
with a deafening roar. A
hum of power started up and the
huge steel disc of the electromagnet
began to twitch . . .

"Woo-hoo!" Zill whooped. "Here we
go!"

Danjo pointed down at SMELL and
the tide of Cyber-Poos with a quivering
pincer. "But here *they* come – straight
for Plog and Furp!"

Plog finished drenching the ground as
his slime-shooter finally ran
dry. Furp threw his own
weapon away as the
last drop dripped
from its nozzle.
Then they looked
up – and gasped.

118

Poo-Poo Prime and his forces were almost on top of them, while SMELL brought up the rear. The marauding mucksters got nearer and nearer. Parp grenade launch pipes rose slowly from their heads.

"All units, fire at my command," droned Poo-Poo Prime.

Plog and Furp watched grimly as the Cyber-Poos sped closer, closer . . . and then began to slow down, as if their ploppy legs were suddenly caught in invisible treacle.

"It's working!" Furp squealed, clapping with excitement as the Cyber-Poos stared down at their stuck feet in confusion and even SMELL strained to keep scraping forwards. "They didn't realize how sticky we'd made the ground."

119

"But they can still get us with their weapons." Poo-Poo Prime fired a parp grenade and Plog quickly kicked it away with a CLANG of metal before it could explode. "See what I mean?"

"You cannot stop us," roared SMELL, his lid snapping open and shut like the jaws of some deadly animal. "Our destiny is to conquer!"

"I'd say your destiny was up in the air, SMELLy-pants!" Plog turned and

shouted up at Zill and Danjo in the crane. "Now, guys – while they're still stuck – hit that mega-magnet!"

Zill heard him and jumped through the air, grabbing hold of a large lever meant for human hands to hold. "Hope this one starts the motor," she gasped, swinging from it. "Oh, no – it won't budge!"

"Let me help!"
Danjo reached up and
pulled on her brushy
tail, helping her drag
down the lever, slowly,
slowly . . .

CLUNK, went the
control. HUMMMMMMM went the
electromagnet as it throbbed into life.

And suddenly, on the ground
below, there was carnage!

Plog turned a
somersault as his metal
boots were yanked
from his feet and shot
like missiles towards
the magnet. Furp
struggled out of his large
metal pants and helmet in
the nick of time as they too
went shooting through the air to cling to
the steel disc dangling high above.

"Phew!" The frog-monster blushed.

"I'm glad I'm wearing clean boxers!"

But the effect on the Cyber-Poos was far more spectacular. With their pooey feet stuck to the ground, their bodies began to stretch as the metal and wires that ran through them were pulled upwards by the penetrating power of the magnet.

"No!" groaned Poo-Poo Prime, his lights flashing as he grew taller and thinner with every passing second. "Noooooooooo!"

At last, with a squelchy, squashy, tearing sound, all the Cyber-Poos' high-tech parts were tugged clean out of their dirty bodies. A storm of circuits, guns and silicon chips went flying through the air – and with a feeble chorus of warbling cries, the Cyber-Poos fell apart into mushy heaps of dung.

"This isn't fair!" SMELL shouted, his casing dragged into the air by the tug of the powerful magnet. "I was going to rule! I was going to be the All-Seeing SMELL!"

"You'll still have a pretty good view from up there," Plog told him.

"You can send Lord Klukk a postcard," Furp added.

BEEP! The shadowy bird-monster's image appeared on SMELL's screen. "What's going on?" he squawked. "I've lost contact with the Cyber-Poos."

"And that's not all, Klukk," Plog shouted. "I think you'll find you've lost *everything*!"

Finally, the electromagnet's hold on SMELL's metal body was too great. With a final shriek that mingled tunelessly with Klukk's roar of frustration, SMELL went shooting upwards into the air and smashed into the

steel disc with enough force to shatter
his casing and blow the poo right out of
his metal body.

Furp hopped up to the driver's cab
and stuck there slimily. "Well done," he
told Zill and Danjo. "Now, kill the
power."

Danjo pushed Zill up in the air and
the lever clonked off again. SMELL's
smoking remains fell to the ground in a
rain of wires and
metal parts,
landing in the
enormous
puddle of
melting
muck.

It was all
that was
left of the
menace of
the Cyber-
Poos.

Danjo slid down from the crane's cab on a slide of slime-ice, holding Zill tightly in his arms. Furp jumped down to join them, and Plog gathered them all up in a big group hug. "We did it!" he cheered.

Furp nodded gravely. "But the biggest challenge is yet to come."

"You mean getting PIE back home?" said Zill. "No sweat – we'll just tie him to a load of balloons and use the Slime-Mobile to tow him back to base."

"And then stick the Big Booster back where we found it," Danjo added.

"No, I did not mean that," said Furp. He looked at the sloppy, stinky pool of poop and metal before them with a sigh. "The biggest challenge will be finding my pants and crash helmet in that revolting muck-pool!"

"And my boots too." Plog looked down at his ugly feet, which were already oozing smelly slime. "Oh, well. At least my tootsies can't smell any worse."

"Ha!" Zill held her nose and grinned. "Well, good luck with that, guys. I think Danjo and I will go and tell PIE the good news – that his Big Booster's safe and he'll soon be back in action."

"And back where he belongs," Danjo agreed. "With his ever-loving team-mates – the Slime Squad!"

Hours later, as the sun began to set over Trashland's curious landscape, a monster passing in the right place at the right time might have witnessed something rather unusual.

A very happy super-computer came floating out of a hole in Silicon Ditch, supported by a flock of seagulls and ninety-nine red balloons. An extremely dirty frog-monster sat on top of the mechanical marvel's monitor, with an equally mucky rat-bear-thing beside him.

"With my Big Booster back, I'll soon be the All-Seeing PIE again," the computer cried, drifting happily through the air. "But I must say, it's nice to get out and see Trashland properly once in a while…"

A thick slime-strand hung down from the computer's base like a towrope, and a skunky poodle monster held it in four paws. A large, red crab-creature with three legs helped her to tie it to an invisible vehicle, and then the whole loopy lot of them zoomed away.

At that moment, far below, in a small village near the Heavy Metal Hills, a little monster and his mum looked up at the incredible sight. "Mummy, mummy!" said the child. "What's THAT?"

"I do believe it's the Slime Squad," said the mum, smiling as the heroic figures faded into the twilight. "Great gonking honk-wobblers – whatever will they get up to next?"

Don't miss the Squaddies in
THE SLIME SQUAD vs
THE SUPERNATURAL SQUID

DON'T MISS THE SLIME SQUAD'S NEXT INCREDIBLE ADVENTURE . . .

Out now!

ENJOY ANOTHER FANTASTIC SLIME SQUAD ADVENTURE . . .

Out now!